Super Spooktacular

BY JESSICA YOUNG
ILLUSTRATED BY JESSICA SECHERET

PICTURE WINDOW BOOKS
a capstone imprint

Finley Flowers is published by Picture Window Books
A Capstone imprint
1710 Roe Crest Drive
North Mankato, Minnesota 56003
www.mycapstone.com

Library of Congress Cataloging-in-Publication Data is
available on the Library of Congress website.

ISBN: 987-1-4795-9807-6 (library hardcover)
ISBN: 978-1-4795-9811-3 (paper over board)
ISBN: 978-1-4795-9827-4 (ebook PDF)
ISBN: 978-1-4795-9831-1 (reflowable epub)

Summary: Finley has to use her creativity to save the
day when her Halloween plans — and costumes — come
unraveled.

Editor: Alison Deering
Designer: Lori Bye

Vector Images: Shutterstock ©

Printed and bound in the USA.
010400F17

For Kate, a super-spooktacular friend

TABLE OF CONTENTS

Chapter 1
HALLOWEEN'S COMING

Finley Flowers got her water bottle out of her cubby and guzzled down the rest of her water. She'd been playing tag when her teacher, Ms. Bird, called the class in from recess. Finley's best friend, Henry Lin, had chased her all the way to the school doors, and she was still trying to catch her breath.

"Everyone take a seat," Ms. Bird said as the rest of the fourth-grade class trickled in from the hall. "We have some exciting things to talk about."

As the students hurried to their desks, Ms. Bird turned on the projector and turned off the lights. Then she pressed a button on the remote. A picture of an orange-and-black butterfly appeared on the board.

"If you've been playing outside lately, you might have spotted one of these," Ms. Bird said. "Can anyone tell me what it is?"

Henry raised his hand. "It's a monarch butterfly. I saw one in our garden."

"Yes!" Ms. Bird's eyes lit up. "Every fall, millions of monarchs take a long journey — up to three thousand miles. In October, they pass through our area on their way to Mexico."

Finley's friend Olivia Snotham raised her hand. "Did you say three *thousand* miles?"

Ms. Bird nodded. "Amazing, isn't it?"

Whoa, Finley thought. *Butterflies are tough.* "How can a tiny butterfly fly that far?" she asked.

"Monarch magic." Ms. Bird pressed the remote, and a chart labeled *Monarch Life Cycle* came up on the board. "Every spring, butterflies from Mexico travel north, stopping to lay their eggs on the undersides of milkweed leaves. When the eggs hatch, the hungry monarch caterpillars munch on the milkweed and grow . . . and grow . . . and grow."

"Like *The Very Hungry Caterpillar*," Henry whispered to Finley. "I loved that book!"

Ms. Bird clicked to the next slide, which showed a picture of a smooth, green pod hanging from a leaf. "The caterpillars form *chrysalises*," she continued, "where they go through some big changes, eventually becoming . . ."

A butterfly stretching its wings appeared on the screen.

"Butterflies!" everyone said together.

Ms. Bird smiled. "Exactly. Then *those* new monarch butterflies continue the journey north and

lay *their* eggs, and the cycle begins again. This series of changes from egg to butterfly is called *metamorphosis*."

"That really is like magic," Finley said.

"Every spring and summer, several generations of butterflies go through this process," Ms. Bird explained. "Each butterfly lives as an adult for an average of four to six weeks. But the fall butterflies are really special."

"Why?" Olivia asked.

Ms. Bird wrote *fall butterflies* on the board. "This generation of butterflies lives for seven to nine *months*. They store extra energy from the nectar they drink on the long trip all the way back to Mexico — the same place their ancestors started the journey. There's not a lot of food for them there, so they'll need that extra energy to survive the winter."

Finley's friend Kate raised her hand. "Wait — if the fall butterflies have never been to Mexico, how do they know where to fly?"

"It's like the monarchs have some type of built-in compass to guide them," Ms. Bird said. "Scientists think that compass tells the butterflies the time of day and the position of the sun so they can find their way south."

"Kind of like the GPS in our car," Henry said.

"Kind of." Ms. Bird pressed the remote. The screen showed a picture of trees covered with butterflies. "After the long journey, the monarchs rest in the mountains. Their heart rates slow, and they huddle together for warmth, clinging to the trees."

"Cool!" Finley exclaimed. "It's like a big butterfly blanket!"

Ms. Bird turned the projector off and the lights on. "We'll spend some more time looking at monarchs. But now for something *almost* as exciting . . ." She paused and gave the class a mysterious look.

"What?" Finley and Olivia said together.

"Monarchs are experts at transformation," Ms. Bird said, walking to the front of the room. "They change from eggs to caterpillars to chrysalises to butterflies." She turned to face the class. "That reminds me — there's a holiday coming up where we can transform ourselves into something new as well . . ."

"Halloween!" the class shouted.

Ms. Bird grinned. "You got it. On Friday, we'll participate in the annual fourth-grade Halloween parade. Now that you're the oldest students at Glendale Elementary, you'll get to strut your stuff and show off your costumes for the rest of the school."

Yes! Finley thought. *We've been in the audience since kindergarten, and now it's our turn to take the stage!*

"We'll also have a class party with snacks and games," Ms. Bird continued, "and a dance floor where you can bust out some monster moves. So come as you aren't — and be prepared to party! I've already picked out my costume."

"What is it?" Finley asked.

"A mermaid?" Kate asked hopefully.

Ms. Bird shook her head.

"A famous artist," Arpin said, "like Frida Kahlo or Georgia O'Keeffe?"

"Nope," Ms. Bird said.

"Einstein?" Henry guessed.

Ms. Bird laughed. "You'll just have to wait and see."

Finley glanced at Henry and did a little dance. She loved school. She loved her teacher and her friends. She loved the smell of freshly sharpened pencils, the art supplies at the craft table, and the reading corner full of pillows and books. She loved learning about amazing things like monarch butterflies. But today she couldn't wait for school to be over — she had a costume to plan! This was going to be the most Fin-tastic Halloween yet!

Chapter 2
WHAT TO WEAR?

"I can't wait for Halloween!" Finley said as she and Henry burst through the school doors that afternoon. "Especially the parade. What are you dressing up as?"

"Elvis," Henry said in his best Elvis voice.

Finley laughed. Henry loved Elvis Presley. He even had a collection of Elvis records.

"I just need to pick a style," Henry continued as they headed toward their street. "There are so many great Elvis looks to choose from."

Finley jumped over a sidewalk crack. "Like what?"

Henry unzipped his backpack and took out his notebook. "I made a list: rockabilly Elvis, army Elvis, cowboy Elvis, Hawaiian Elvis, karate Elvis . . . but since it's Halloween, I think I might be *vampire* Elvis."

"Wow," Finley said. "I didn't know Elvis was a vampire."

Henry grinned. "He wasn't. But he would have made a great one."

"I can totally see you as vampire Elvis," Finley said. She scooped up a leaf and twirled it between her fingers. "What kind of costume should I make? Something funny? Or scary? Or wild? I can't decide."

"Well," Henry said, "last year you were a carrot."

Finley frowned. "Don't remind me. I could barely walk with all that stuffing. And the green hairspray took forever to wash out. You should have stopped me."

Henry shrugged. "It seemed like a good idea at the time. No one had the same costume as you. And carrots are your favorite vegetable."

"This year I'm going to be the opposite of a carrot," Finley said. "Something with sparkle. Something spooktacular! I just have to figure out what that something is."

Finley and Henry crunched through the leaves. They came to a stop in front of Finley's house.

"I gotta go," Henry said. "I have soccer. But don't worry — I know you'll think up a Fin-tastic costume. You've got so many idea seeds in your head. The right one just hasn't sprouted yet."

"Let's hope it hurries," Finley said. "I only have until Friday."

After waving goodbye to Henry, Finley let herself in the front door. She hung up her jacket and dumped her backpack on one of the dining room chairs.

"Hey, I'm trying to work here." Finley's older brother, Zack, pointed to the homework spread out in front of him.

Finley ignored him. "Guess what?" she said. "I get to have a Halloween party and a costume parade at school this week!"

Zack grabbed an apple from the bowl on the table. "I remember the fourth-grade costume parade. Make sure you wear something good. The whole school will be watching. What are you going to be for Halloween this year — broccoli?"

Finley scowled. "Very funny. At least *I* dressed up last year."

"I dressed up too," Zack said, chomping on his apple. "I was a baseball player."

Finley raised an eyebrow. "You wore your own baseball uniform — you basically went as yourself. And the year before that you stuck one googly eye on your forehead and said you were an ogre."

"So?" Zack said. "What's wrong with that?"

"You couldn't even see the googly eye. Your hair covered it up."

"Well, this year I'm not dressing up," Zack said matter-of-factly.

"Why not?" Finley asked.

"Too old."

Finley laughed. "That's ridiculous. Even grown-ups dress up. Look at Mom and Dad. They've been Zeus and Hera, Green Eggs and Ham, a rainbow and a unicorn . . ."

Zack shook his head. "That's different. They dress up for *us*. They wouldn't do it if we weren't around."

"That's not true," Finley said. "They like it."

"I just don't see the point. Why pretend to be something you're not?"

Finley sighed. "Because it's *fun*. And what about trick-or-treating? You can't go trick-or-treating if you don't dress up."

Zack shrugged. "I don't want to trick-or-treat."

"Fine," Finley said. "But don't expect me to share my candy."

"I'll have plenty of candy," Zack said, smirking. "I'll be the one giving it out."

Finley rolled her eyes. Grabbing one of the Halloween mail-order catalogs from the counter, she marched upstairs to her room. She flopped onto her bed and leafed through the pages. There were costumes of angels, monsters, superheroes, villains, movie characters, and ten different types of witches. But somehow they all looked the same.

Finley frowned as she came to a section labeled
BOY COSTUMES. *Since when is an astronaut a boy
costume?* she wondered. It almost made her want to
be one just to prove them wrong. But an astronaut
didn't have the sparkle she was looking for.

Tossing the catalog down, Finley pulled out her
craft box from under her bed and rummaged through
it. She found origami paper, pipe cleaners, beads of
every size and color, a kajillion pencils that needed
sharpening . . . but no ideas.

Maybe I'll organize my art stuff, she thought. *That way, when Fin-spiration strikes, I'll be ready.*

* * *

By the time Dad called Finley to dinner, she'd organized everything in her craft box. Her markers were arranged in rainbow order. Her papers were stacked. Her stickers were sorted. But she still hadn't thought of a spooktacular costume.

Finley was just sitting down at the table when her little sister, Evie, came skipping into the kitchen.

"Something smells good," Evie said as she twirled on tiptoes toward her chair.

"Have a seat," Zack said. "You're making me dizzy."

"Four more days till Halloween!" Evie announced. "We need to get decorations — and treats!" She plunked down in her chair, gulped some milk, and turned to Dad. "Remember those leaf hammocks

Finley made for her class art project? You said we could make some in the yard."

Dad raised an eyebrow. "I did?"

Evie nodded. "You said we could put mummies in them."

Dad made his trying-to-remember face. "I *did*?"

"Yep." Zack said. "I believe you said we'd have the best-decorated house in the neighborhood."

Mom laughed. "Well, I guess we'd better get started."

"We need pumpkins," Finley reminded her.

"I'm going to a pumpkin patch!" Evie said. "We're taking a field trip to a real farm with hayrides and a corn maze!" She stirred her soup and sipped a drippy spoonful.

"I remember Puckett's Pick-Your-Own Pumpkin Patch," Zack said. "We went there in second grade. Don't get lost in the corn maze — it's haunted."

"Haunted?" Evie put her spoon down.

"Zack." Mom gave him a knock-it-off look as she set a bowl of salad and a plate of rolls on the table.

Zack reached for a roll. "That's what my friend Sam said. He got separated from the group. And when he finally caught up, he was all out of breath. He said a ghost was chasing him."

"*Zack.*" Mom shot him a warning look. "Why don't you go ahead and eat?"

"Just trying to help," Zack said.

Mom turned to Evie and smiled. "Don't worry, doodlebug. The pumpkin patch will be *great*."

"Mom's right," Finley added. "You're lucky — you get to pick out your own pumpkin to keep. Plus, the corn maze is fun — and it's *not* haunted."

Evie glanced at Finley then went back to slurping her soup. "I don't care if it is," she said, jutting out her chin in Zack's direction. "Ghosts are cool. Besides, with my costume, they'll be more scared of me than I am of them."

"What are you going to be?" Finley asked.

"It's a secret," Evie said. "What are *you* going to be?"

Finley shrugged. She wished she knew.

Chapter 3
A SUPERNOVA IS BORN

The next day after school, Henry came over to Finley's house to help her brainstorm costume ideas. Halloween was three days away, and she was still stumped.

"Let's get a snack before we get down to business," Finley said. She was poking around in the fridge when Evie leaped through the door.

"Hey, Evie," Henry said as she streaked by. "What's up?"

"I'm getting ready for Halloween," Evie said, dancing across the kitchen and striking a pose. "Guess what I'm going to be."

Henry shrugged. "Um . . . a ballerina?"

Evie shook her head. "Nope." She tiptoed past Finley, curtsied, and leaped back out the doorway.

"She's been acting stranger than usual," Finley whispered as she handed Henry a glass of juice.

Henry raised an eyebrow. "How so?"

"She keeps flitting around like a nervous bird, and this morning she wouldn't stop following me."

"Maybe Halloween has her spooked," Henry said.

"Not a chance. She loves Halloween — it's her favorite holiday." Finley arranged some cheese and crackers on a plate. "Want to see if there are any good shows on while we eat our snacks?"

"Sure. Then we'll think up a spooktacular costume for you."

Finley and Henry headed into the living room and settled onto the sofa. Finley had just flipped to the science channel when Evie wandered in with a bag of crackers.

"What are you guys doing?" she asked.

"Watching a show on space," Finley said, her eyes fixed on the screen.

"Cool." Without waiting for an invite, Evie squeezed in between Finley and Henry and crunched her crackers. "Is it for school?"

"No," Finley said. "It just looked interesting."

"Maybe we could watch *The Mew Crew*," Evie said hopefully.

"No thanks." Finley brushed Evie's cracker crumbs off her jeans. "Why don't you get a plate?"

Evie popped the last cracker into her mouth. "Dats otay. I'b aw dum."

Just then, the music from the show got louder. The animated solar system on the screen transformed into a brilliant, multicolored light.

Finley leaned in closer and turned up the volume. "Whoa. What is *that*?"

"A supernova is a dying star that explodes in a sudden burst of energy," a woman's voice on the show explained. "As the massive star runs out of fuel, it collapses under its own weight, then bounces back in an enormous explosion. The temperature inside an exploding supernova can reach billions of degrees."

"A dying star," Henry said. "That's awesome."

"That *is* awesome," Finley agreed. "And I just thought of an awesome idea for my costume — a super-sparkly, super-spooktacular supernova!"

Henry grinned. "If anyone has enough energy to be a supernova, it's you. But how will you make the costume?"

"I'll figure something out," Finley said. "Now that I have the perfect idea, that part will be a breeze."

* * *

After the show, Henry went home for dinner. Finley wolfed down some mac and cheese and got to work on her math homework. She'd just finished her last word problem when the doorbell rang. It was Henry.

"Hey," he said. "Long time no see." He unzipped his backpack and handed her a book. "We were out for a bike ride, so I brought you something."

Finley read the title. *"Universe."* She pointed to the picture of a galaxy on the cover. "It's like that cool show we watched."

Henry nodded. "There's a whole chapter on supernovae. I thought it might help with your costume. It's my mom's. She had it from a college class she took. She said you can borrow it as long as you want."

"You're the best," Finley said. "I can't wait to read it." She waved to Henry's mom, who was waiting on the sidewalk. "Tell her thanks for me."

"I will," Henry said, heading back to his bike.

Finley took the book to her room and flipped through the pages. *Supernovae sure are beautiful*, she thought. *Look at all those swirling colors.*

She rifled through her drawers and pulled out some black leggings and a matching long-sleeved shirt. Then she ran to the kitchen, where Mom and Dad were finishing the dishes.

"Can I use these for my costume?" Finley asked, holding up the clothes. "I need to paint them."

"Sure. Hold on a minute." Mom disappeared down the hall, then came back with a clear plastic package and handed it to Finley. "Here."

Finley looked it over. "A shower curtain?"

"You can use it as a drop cloth to catch any spills," Mom said. "In fact, why don't you paint on the porch?"

"Good idea," Finley said. "Thanks!" She threw on her sweater, grabbed her craft box, and headed outside.

On the porch, Finley unfolded the shower curtain and spread it out. She laid the leggings and shirt on top of it. Dipping a paintbrush into some sparkly neon paint, she sprinkled the clothes with a shower of streaks and dots.

Next she sifted through her art stuff and fished out some multicolored jewels. *These will add some pizzazz,* she thought, gluing them in place.

Leaving her outfit to dry, Finley went back inside to get Henry's *Universe* book from her desk. She sat on the sofa and turned to the picture of a supernova. It didn't look anything like her costume.

It's so shimmery and glimmery, she thought. *I need some serious sparkle.*

Finley knew just what to do. It was time to call a sparkle expert. She grabbed the phone and dialed Olivia's number.

"Hi," she said when Olivia answered. "What are you doing?"

"Putting the finishing touches on my fortune-teller costume," Olivia said. "I got an awesome wig and a lace shawl and a real crystal ball. I'm ready for the parade! And my cousin's having a birthday party on Halloween night. I predict it's going to be amazing! What are you doing?"

"Reading a book about the universe. Henry let me borrow it to research my costume."

"You're going to be the universe for Halloween?"

Finley laughed. "No, I'm going to be a supernova."

"Oh," Olivia said. "What's a supernova?"

"It's basically an exploding star."

"Whoa. What are you going to wear?"

"I'm not sure yet," Finley said, "but it has to be something with sparkle. I was hoping you might be able to help."

"I definitely know sparkle," Olivia said. "Why don't I come over tomorrow for a consultation? I'll bring some supplies and get you fixed right up."

"That would be great," Finley said.

"Perfect!" Olivia replied. "My mom can drop me off. Don't worry — you'll be ready to shine in no time!"

Chapter 4
SPARKLIFIED

When Olivia's mom pulled into the driveway the next afternoon, Finley was waiting at the door.

"Thanks for coming to the rescue," she said as Olivia lugged her purple suitcase up the porch steps.

"No worries." Olivia waved goodbye to her mom and stepped inside. "You can always count on me in a costume emergency."

"Come on," Finley said, heading upstairs. "I'll show you what I've got so far."

Olivia followed Finley to her room. The paint-splattered shirt and leggings lay on the shower curtain on her floor. Finley tugged them on, and Olivia looked them over.

"This is great for a base layer," Olivia said, "but you definitely need more glitz." She heaved her suitcase onto the bed. "Luckily, I have just the thing."

"What's in there?" Finley asked.

Olivia lifted the lid. "Treasure."

Finley leaned in to examine the tangled pile of accessories. "Wow! That's a lot of sparkle."

Olivia nodded. "Sparkle is my specialty." She dug through the suitcase and pulled out a gold, sequined scarf. "Here," she said, handing it to Finley.

Finley took the scarf and tied it around her head. "How do you wear it? Like this?"

Olivia giggled. "Try it this way instead." She untied the scarf and draped it around Finley's shoulders. "There. You look more like a supernova already — a very *glamorous* supernova."

"I like it," Finley said, checking out her reflection in the mirror.

"Sparkle never goes out of style," Olivia said. "Wait till you see how those sequins reflect the light."

Finley turned to Olivia. "That's it!" she said. "We need light!"

Just then, Mom poked her head through the door. "Hi, Olivia. How are you?"

"Sparkly," Olivia answered.

"Mom," Finley said, "remember those twinkly lights we used to decorate the table at your book club dinner?"

Mom nodded. "They looked great — everyone loved them."

"Could I use them for my costume?" Finley asked. "The package said they were wearable."

Mom shrugged. "I don't see why not. I'll try to find them."

Finley and Olivia went back to looking through the glittery treasures. They tried on crystal-studded bangles, beaded necklaces, and metallic belts.

"What about this?" Olivia held up a rhinestone tiara. "It would look fabulous with twinkly lights."

Before Finley could reply, there was a knock on the door. Mom appeared with a plastic storage bin.

"I think the lights are in here," she said, setting it down. "You can put it back in the basement when you're done."

"Thanks!" Finley rummaged through the plastic tub and found two strands of tiny, battery-powered lights. They twinkled like fireflies when she switched them on.

"Perfect!" Olivia said. "I just wish you had more."

"Me too. But two is better than none." Finley snapped the lid onto the plastic bin. "Come on, let's put this back."

Olivia trailed Finley to the top of the basement steps. "It's spooky down there," she said, peering down the stairs.

"Don't worry," Finley said, leading the way. "We won't stay long."

As Finley plunked the bin down and turned to go, she spotted her bike parked in the corner. "Hey," she said, unclipping a bike light from her handlebars, "maybe I could wear this." She flicked the switch on the side, and it flashed red and orange.

"Brilliant!" Olivia said.

"And look" — Finley pointed to the rest of the family's bikes — "we've got lots more!" She unclipped the lights from the handlebars and seat posts and carried them upstairs.

"Can I use these bike lights for my costume?" Finley asked Mom as they passed through the kitchen.

"You can use them," Mom said. "Just don't lose them."

"Thanks!" Finley called as she and Olivia bounded up the stairs to her room.

"The lights are perfect," Olivia said, "but how are you going to wear them?"

Finley knelt beside her costume and ran a hand over the paint-flecked shower curtain. "Maybe we could use this to make some kind of see-through skirt," she said. "We could fold it over like a pocket and put the twinkly lights inside."

Olivia raised her eyebrows. "That just might work."

Finley cut off the top of the shower curtain then folded it in half. Olivia cut slits in the top edges and wove one of her belts in and out. Then she held up the see-through skirt while Finley spread the twinkling lights between the plastic layers.

When they were done, Finley wrapped the skirt around her waist. She buckled the belt and clipped the bike lights around the top.

"Not bad," she said, swishing this way and that.

"One more thing." Olivia pulled out a package of fiber-optic hair clips. She turned them on, and they pulsed with glowing colors as she arranged them in Finley's hair.

"Thanks!" Finley said. Then she turned out the lights and spun around. "How do I look?"

"Like a supernova!" Olivia said. She handed Finley a can of glitter hairspray and a bunch of glow sticks. "And with this stardust spray and some glow sticks, you'll be dazzling."

"You're the best!" Finley said, giving Olivia a hug. She couldn't wait for the costume parade. She was going to be a star!

Chapter 5
BLING FOR THE KING

The next day, Finley walked home with Henry to check out his costume.

"So, tell me why you like Elvis so much," she said, kicking a stray pebble down the sidewalk.

"Because . . ." Henry got his hard-thinking face. "He's Elvis!"

Finley laughed. "I need more details," she said.

"Hold on," Henry said. "I've got a list." He pulled his notebook out of his pocket and flipped through it.

Finley smiled. Henry had a list for everything.

"Here," he said, handing the notebook to Finley.

Five Reasons Why I Like Elvis:

He took gospel, country, jazz, and blues and mixed them up to make something new — like a really great musical recipe.

He taught himself to sing and play guitar.

He didn't give up, even when people said he'd never make it.

He started as an unknown kid and turned himself into The King of Rock 'n Roll.

His favorite sandwich was fried peanut butter and banana.

Finley read the list. "Wow, she said." I have a new appreciation for The King." She handed the notebook back. "I can't wait to see your costume."

Finley loved going to Henry's house. She always thought it looked like the cottage in one of her fairytale books. As they walked up the path to the back door, she spotted something orange in the garden.

"Are those pumpkins?" she asked, pointing to the smooth globes peeking out from a tangle of vines.

"Those are squash," Henry said. He opened the garden gate and slipped through. Finley followed as he tiptoed down the rows.

Henry stopped and pushed back some broad leaves. "*These* are pumpkins."

"Whoa," Finley said. "They're humungous!"

"Pretty cool, huh?" Henry patted one, and it made a dull thud. "I can't wait to make pumpkin soup."

"Yum!" Finley said. "I can't wait to taste it."

Finley and Henry picked their way through the garden to the house.

"Hi, Mom!" Henry called into the garage. "Finley's here!"

"Hi!" Mrs. Lin answered. "I'm fixing my bike — I'll be in soon."

Henry and Finley let themselves in through the back door and kicked off their shoes. Grabbing a bag from the counter, Henry emptied it onto the kitchen table.

"Check it out," he said. "I've got gold sunglasses, a cape, blue suede shoes, fangs, hair gel — I even found stick-on sideburns." He held up a package with two black strips of hair. "What do you think?"

Finley grinned. "I think you're going to rock."

"I hope so." Henry played air guitar and struck a pose. "I'm *The King of Rock and Roll!*"

Finley laughed. "You look great," she said. "But The King needs some bling."

"What kind of bling?" Henry asked.

"Sparkly stuff," Finley said. "Didn't Elvis wear some flashy outfits?"

Henry nodded. "He had a special sense of style."

Suddenly, Finley felt an idea sprouting. Olivia had helped her — now it was her turn to help. "I can sparklify your cape!" she said. "I've got tons of fake jewels left over from my costume. It'll be Hen-sational!"

"That would be good," Henry said. "But I've got a soccer game. We probably only have twenty minutes. How long will sparklifying take?"

Finley frowned. "Longer than that. Plus, all of the stuff is at my house. Why don't you give me your costume? I'll bring it to school with mine tomorrow. We can change for the party when we get there."

Henry raised an eyebrow. "Will you be really, *really* careful with it?"

Finley crossed her heart. "I'll guard it with my life."

"All right," Henry said. He put all of his costume stuff back into the bag and handed it to Finley. "Just don't forget it. And not too much bling."

"Too much bling?" Finley shook her head. "No such thing." She turned to go.

"Hey, hold on a sec," Henry said. He disappeared into the garage then came back holding a small set of garden shears. "Want to come choose a pumpkin?"

"Really?" Finley's eyes lit up.

Henry nodded. "Mom says we've got lots."

"Thanks, Mrs. Lin!" Finley called into the garage.

Henry's mom appeared at the door with a bike wheel in her hand. "You're welcome," she said. "Get a good one!"

Finley and Henry walked to the middle of the garden. "Pick a pumpkin," Henry said, "any pumpkin."

Finley bent down to examine her options. She compared colors and stems. She felt leathery leaves and ran her hands over ridges and bumps.

"This is the biggest one," Henry said, patting a squat, round pumpkin.

"You should keep it," Finley said. She pointed to a tall, lop-sided one in the middle row. "I like that one."

Henry carefully cut the stem and handed the pumpkin to Finley.

"Thanks!" she said, sliding the handle of Henry's costume bag onto her wrist. "Mom and Dad didn't get our pumpkins yet. I was starting to worry I wouldn't have one this year."

"Are you okay to walk home with it?" Henry asked. "It's heavy."

"No problem." Finley flexed her arm and made a muscle. "Good luck with your game! I'll see you tomorrow."

When Finley got home, she set the pumpkin down and went upstairs to take care of Henry's costume. She spread the cape out on the floor of her room. Then she picked all the gold jewels out of her craft box and arranged them into a giant *E* in the center. After gluing each jewel in place, she added zigzag lines of sequins to make it look like the *E* was shining.

That's some bling worthy of The King, Finley thought, admiring her handiwork. She couldn't wait to show Henry.

Next, Finley laid her own costume out on the bed and double-checked that it was all there: shirt and leggings, light-up skirt, fiber-optic barrettes, glow sticks, and stardust spray.

After making sure the glue on the jewels was dry, Finley placed Henry's gold sunglasses, fake sideburns, hair gel, fangs, and blue suede shoes in the middle of his cape. She wrapped them up carefully. Then she tucked both costumes into her gym bag and set it by the front door.

One more sleep till Halloween! Finley thought. *And we're ready for our transformation!*

Chapter 6
DISAPPEARING ACT

On Halloween morning, Finley woke up extra early. She made her bed, got dressed, ate breakfast, and brushed her teeth. Then she sat on the couch reading Henry's *Universe* book while she waited for Mom and Evie. She was just starting the chapter on black holes when Evie bounded down the stairs in a tattered tutu and growled.

"I thought you weren't going to be a ballerina," Finley said.

"I'm not a ballerina!" Evie roared. "I'm a *zombie* ballerina! Lucy's going to be one too. I'm going to her house after school. I've got extra zombie clothes and makeup in here." She held up her gym bag, which matched Finley's. "We're all set for the field trip."

"Whoa!" Zack said as he came around the corner. "That's something I didn't expect to see." He leaned in for a closer look. "What's all over your face?"

Evie grinned. "Lipstick. Mom let me use her makeup to draw scars and blood and zombie stuff."

"Ew," Zack said, wrinkling his nose.

Evie shrieked and started zombie-dancing after him as he scrambled over the couch.

"Girls, we're leaving in five minutes!" Mom called from upstairs. "Zack, you'd better hurry, or you'll miss the bus!"

"Okay!" Zack answered, grabbing his backpack. He turned to Finley. "Have fun being broccoli or whatever your costume is." Then he tugged Evie's tutu. "Scare lots of humans — and watch out for ghosts."

Finley and Evie gathered their things and headed for the car. Mom hurried after them, juggling her briefcase, an armful of books, and her coffee. Finley nestled her costume bag into the trunk and climbed into the back seat.

Evie tossed her bag next to Finley's, slammed the trunk shut, and leaped in after her. Then she checked her zombie makeup in the flip-down mirror. "Aaargh!" she groaned, making a scary face and pawing at Finley's leg.

Finley fake-screamed and clawed at the window. She couldn't wait to get out of the car and into her own costume.

By the time they arrived at school, Finley was extra hoppity. She knew Henry would be waiting for her. He was always on time.

"Don't forget your bags," Mom said, popping the trunk. "Evie, remember you're riding home from the field trip with Lucy. I'll pick you up at her house later."

Evie leaped out of the car and grabbed her bag. "Bye!" she called, lugging her stuff up the front walk to the school doors.

Finley got her bag and waved goodbye to Mom. Then she followed Evie inside and speed-walked down the hall.

Sure enough, Henry was waiting by the cubbies. "Happy Halloween!" he called.

Finley grinned. "Happy Halloween to you!"

Together they hung up their jackets and stood in the classroom doorway. The lights were dimmed, and fake candles shone in clusters all around the room. A huge spider web stretched across the back wall, and bats and paper jack-o'-lanterns dangled from the ceiling. Ms. Bird had written *EAT, DRINK, AND BE SCARY!* on the board in drippy-looking, black letters.

"Wow," Finley said. "The room looks great!"

"Look — Ms. Bird is a witch!" Henry pointed to the life-sized dummy propped up in the teacher's chair.

Glancing around, Finley spotted a Dalmatian, two superheroes, a pirate, a wizard, a football player, a doctor, and an alien. Their friends Lia and Kate were both dressed as witches, with matted black wigs and black lips and nails to match.

"Let's get changed," Henry said. "I can't wait to see my cape!"

As they headed for the door, Olivia waved Finley over.

"Hey, Olivia!" Finley said. "I like your crystal ball. We'll be right back — we're going to get changed."

Olivia narrowed her eyes. "Who is this *Olivia* you speak of?" she said in a mysterious voice. "I am Madame Fortuna, fortune teller extraordinaire."

"Excellent," said Henry. "Can you tell me my fortune?"

Olivia put out her hand. "That will be one treat, please — and I only take chocolate."

"I'm fresh out of chocolate," Henry said.

Olivia sighed. "Fine. You can owe me." She rubbed her temples and stared at the crystal ball on her desk. "Now, I must focus."

As Finley and Henry watched, Olivia scrunched her eyebrows together and waved her hands around the crystal ball.

"Madame Fortuna predicts that soon you will not be yourself," she said to Henry. "In a very short time, you will be totally transformed. As for you," she said, turning to Finley, "your future looks very, *very* bright."

Henry smirked. "Thanks, Madame Fortuna. Your powers of prediction are amazing."

Olivia nodded solemnly. "Madame Fortuna knows all."

Finley turned to Henry. "Ready for operation transformation?" she asked, patting her bag.

Henry nodded. "As Elvis would say, 'It's Now or Never.' I can't wait to put on my '*Boo* Suede Shoes' and cape!"

They stepped into the hallway, and Finley unzipped her bag. But when she reached in, instead of Henry's cape, her fingers found a plastic bottle.

"Bug spray?" she said. "What's that doing in here?" She rooted around and pulled out some mosquito netting, granola bars, marshmallows, a ripped sweater and jeans, and a roll of toilet paper.

"I don't get it," she said. "Our costumes were in here — but now they're gone!"

Chapter 7
THINK FAST

"Gone?" Henry's voice cracked. "What do you mean gone?"

"I put our costumes in here last night," Finley said, feeling around inside the bag once more just to be sure. "Someone must have taken them."

"Who would steal homemade Halloween costumes and leave all of this other stuff?" Henry asked.

As Finley started repacking the bag, she spotted a tube of bright red lipstick. Then it hit her. "Oh, no."

"What?"

"This is Evie's bag." Finley whispered. "Not mine."

Henry crinkled his brow. "Well, where's your bag?"

Finley felt faint. She tried to think, but it was like her brain was working in slow motion. "Probably at Puckett's Pick-Your-Own Pumpkin Patch with Evie," she said. "Our gym bags look the same. She must have grabbed mine by mistake."

Henry glared. "I thought you were going to guard my costume with your life!"

"I was — I mean, I did!" Finley's heart raced. "Just give me a minute. I'll think of something."

But Finley didn't know what to do. Evie's field trip would last all day, and then she was going straight to Lucy's. By that time the Halloween party and parade would be long over.

Henry slouched against the wall. "I was ready to 'Rock Around the Clock,'" he muttered. "But now 'I'm All Shook Up.'"

"Hold on." Finley zipped up the bag and heaved it onto her shoulder. "Maybe they haven't left yet!" She bolted down the hall with Henry on her heels.

If we can catch them before they leave, I can switch bags with Evie, Finley thought. *Everything will be okay.*

She sprinted past the third-grade classrooms, the bag bumping against her side. Her shoes squeaked on the polished floors as she tore around the corner to the second-grade hall and skidded to a stop outside the door marked *Ms. Patel's Class.*

Finley knocked. There was no answer.

She opened the door a crack and peeked in. The lights were off. The class was empty.

She ran to the window, hoping to see the field trip buses still parked outside. But they were gone.

"Great," Henry said from behind her. "The party's already started. The parade is in half an hour. And my vampire Elvis costume has left the building. We are officially costume-less on Halloween."

Finley glanced over her shoulder at Henry. He looked like a deflated balloon. "It's all my fault," she said. "I'm sorry."

Henry sighed. "It's okay. We'll just have to sit this one out."

"It's *not* okay." Finley paced around the room. "There's got to be *something* we can use for a costume."

"We could wear that map of the world," Henry said, pointing to the far wall. "Although Ms. Patel might not appreciate us taking it down."

Finley mustered a smile. "Probably not."

"Or we could go as clones of ourselves," Henry suggested. "Then we wouldn't need costumes."

"That sounds like something Zack would do." Finley unzipped Evie's bag. "Maybe there's something in here we can use."

She dumped the contents of the bag out on the floor and sorted through them. "Bug spray, a whistle, mosquito netting, a flashlight, granola bars, lipstick, marshmallows, garlic . . . *garlic?* Why was Evie carrying all this stuff around?"

"Who knows?" Henry said. "I just hope she doesn't need it. Especially this — think fast!"

He picked up a roll of toilet paper and threw it at Finley. It hit her on the leg and tumbled across the floor, unrolling as it went.

Finley chased after it and started wrapping it up. She was almost to the end of the roll when she stopped in her tracks.

"I've got it!" she said, turning to Henry. "Quick — come here!"

"What are you going to do?" Henry asked, raising an eyebrow.

Finley held up the toilet paper roll. "I'm going to make you a mummy. Then you can make me one too."

Henry backed away. "You want to wrap my body in toilet paper? No thanks. I'd rather be a carrot."

"It's time for a transformation," Finley said. "We came in this classroom as you and me, and we're going out as mummies."

Henry shook his head. "Correction — *you* are going out as a mummy."

Finley frowned. "Come on, don't give up! I'm really sorry about the bag mix-up, but now we have another chance. We can still be in the parade!"

Henry hesitated for a minute. Then he groaned. "Fine. Let's try it. Any costume is better than no costume."

Finley grinned and grabbed anothe roll from Evie's bag. "That's the spirit! Commence Operation Mummification!"

"More like Operation Humiliation," Henry muttered.

Finley ignored him. "You can go first." She squirted sanitizer from the dispenser on the wall into her hand and went to rub it on Henry's shirt. "Stand still."

Henry jumped back. "What are you doing?"

"It's anti-bacterial," Finley explained. "I'm preparing the body. That's what you do for mummies, right? You're the one who loves ancient Egypt."

Henry laughed. "This isn't ancient Egypt, and I'm not a real mummy — let's just stick to wrapping."

"Suit yourself." Finley unrolled the toilet paper and circled it around the top of Henry's head. "Turn, turn, turn."

Finley wrapped as Henry turned in place. The toilet paper clung in overlapping layers. She wrapped his arms, his legs, and back up to his head, leaving a space for his eyes.

"Are you almost done?" Henry asked. "I'm getting dizzy."

"Don't get so *wound* up," Finley said.

"Ha," Henry mumbled. "Easy for you to say."

"Just one more turn and . . . ta-daaaah!" Finley beamed. "My very first mummy! Move over, King Tut!"

Henry held his arms out in front of him. "Huh," he said. "You're a pretty good wrapper. Is this your first mummification?"

Finley nodded. "I must be a natural." She handed Henry the toilet paper. "Now it's your turn."

Henry held it up. "Let's rock and *roll*!"

As Finley spun in place, Henry copied her technique, wrapping her from head to toe.

"We'd better *wrap* it up," Finley said, "or we'll miss the party!"

"Done!" Henry said.

Finley grabbed the gym bag. "Let's not tell anyone who we are," she said as they slipped out of Evie's classroom and closed the door behind them. "We'll be mystery mummies!"

Henry put a finger to his lips. "Mum's the word."

Chapter 8
OPERATION MUMMIFICATION

Finley and Henry tiptoed back to class. As they got closer, Finley heard music and laughter. She paused outside the door and turned to Henry. "Ready?"

Henry nodded. "Ready."

The toilet-papered twosome slunk into the classroom. They were headed for the snack table when Olivia intercepted them.

"There you are," she said to Finley. "What happened to your costume? Where's all the sparkle?"

Finley sighed. "Evie accidentally took our real costumes to Puckett's Pick-Your-Own Pumpkin Patch."

Olivia rolled her eyes. "Are you serious?"

"Unfortunately, yes," Henry said. "How did you know it was us?"

"Madame Fortuna knows all." Olivia wiggled her eyebrows. "Actually, one of Finley's braids is showing. And everyone else was already here."

"Well, if you could keep our identities under *wraps*, that would be great," Henry said.

"You got it," Olivia said. "I'm sorry about your costumes. But at least you have a Plan B." She leaned in and examined Finley's arm. "Is that *toilet paper*?"

Finley nodded. "We prefer to call it *wrapping* paper."

Just then Arpin walked by dressed as an alien. "Hi, Henry!" he said, his eye stalks bobbing.

Henry sighed. "So much for our secret. I guess we're not as mysterious as we thought."

"Come on, mummies." Olivia grabbed Finley and Henry's hands. "Let's hit the dance floor." She steered them toward the back of the classroom, where the desks had been pushed aside. A disco ball hung from the ceiling.

"Look — it's the real Ms. Bird!" Finley said, pointing. "She's a magician, not a witch."

Ms. Bird was standing in the corner, arranging caramel apples, fruit, and bags of popcorn on pumpkin-shaped platters. She was dressed all in black, with a top hat, cape, and gloves.

"I bet she's got some fun tricks up her sleeve," Olivia said as she led Finley and Henry to the middle of the dance floor.

"Let's *boo*-gie down!" Henry said, showing off his dance moves. "Check it out — the swim! The sprinkler! The twist! And my personal favorite: the mummy!" He put his arms straight out in front of him and rocked from side to side.

"Where'd you learn those moves?" Olivia asked.

"My mummy," Henry said. "We have after-dinner dance parties while we do the dishes."

Finley, Henry, and Olivia took turns playing dance-floor follow the leader. Soon Kate, Lia, and their friend Will joined in.

"Robot!" Kate yelled, jerking her arms and legs around.

"Stir the pot!" Lia made a giant stirring motion.

"Moonwalk!" Henry slid backward across the floor.

"Monster mash!" Finley bumped her fists together.

By the time Ms. Bird called everyone to recess, Finley and her friends were hot and sweaty.

"Whew," Henry said. "I need to cool off. My mummy wrap is starting to stick."

As the class streamed out of the school doors, Olivia glanced at the sky. "Madame Fortuna predicts it will soon rain."

Henry eyed the dark, billowing clouds. "Nah," he said. "Those are just for decoration — it's Halloween."

"Come on!" Kate tugged on Finley's hand. "We're playing witch tag. If the witch tags you with her wand, you turn into an animal until someone sets you free by touching you and yelling the magic word."

"What's the magic word?" Finley asked.

"*Toad juice*," Kate said.

Henry raised an eyebrow. "That's two words."

Kate shrugged. "The witch picks the word. Lia is the witch, and she picked *toad juice*."

Finley, Henry, and Olivia followed Kate to the far corner of the soccer field. Lia was waving her wand around, chasing after Will.

"Aaaah!" Will yelled, hopping toward Finley. "No more witch tag! I'm tired of being a frog!"

"Let's play Franken-tag," Henry suggested.

"How do you play that?" Will asked, panting.

"It's the same as regular tag, but everyone has to walk like this." Henry demonstrated his best Frankenstein walk, lumbering over to tag Finley.

Finley spun around and staggered after him, arms waving. "HENRY! HEEEENRYYY!" she moaned. Then she swiveled and tagged Olivia.

They were right in the middle of the game when it started to pour. As the rain pelted down, everyone bolted for the school doors.

"I told you it would rain!" Olivia yelled over her shoulder. "Madame Fortuna knows all!"

Finley and Henry raced across the field. Finley could feel her toilet paper tearing off in long, soggy strips.

"I'm melting!" Henry cried as they reached the basketball court.

Finley flung the school door open and leaped inside. But it was too late.

"Great," she said, tugging at the tattered wrapping on her arm. "Now we look like mummies who've been through a car wash."

Henry pulled a nest of waterlogged toilet paper off his head and watched it drip onto the floor. "Ew. There goes Plan B."

"Uh-oh," Olivia said. "The mummies are disintegrating."

Finley peeled off what was left of her mummy wrap. "Come on, Madame Fortuna, can't you cast a spell and make our real costumes appear?"

Olivia shook her head. "I'm a fortune teller, not a wizard. I'm no good at *spell*ing."

"Ha! Nice one." Henry balled up his shredded layers and aimed at the trash can.

Ms. Bird rang the chime to get everyone's attention. "The costume parade starts in ten minutes," she said. "Make sure you're ready to strut your stuff."

Henry looked at Finley. "All our plans have unraveled! What are we going to do?"

Chapter 9
METAMORPHOSIS

"We need some Halloween magic." Finley's eyes darted around the class and came to rest on the monarch butterfly display.

I wish we were butterflies, she thought. *Then we could fly away.*

Suddenly, Finley felt the tickle of an idea sprouting. She spun around to face Henry. "Time for a costume change!"

"Again?" Henry and Olivia said together.

Finley grabbed some pipe cleaners from the craft table and twisted two of them to form a circle. Then she attached two more so they stuck straight up and placed the circle on Henry's head.

Henry crinkled his brow. "Um, what kind of costume is this?"

"A monarch butterfly costume!" Finley exclaimed. "We just need wings."

"Brilliant!" Henry said. "We could make wings out of construction paper."

Olivia shook her head. "You need something bigger."

Finley's eyes lit up. "Like the mosquito netting in Evie's bag!" She dragged the bag over and dug out the gauzy fabric.

"Spread your arms," she told Henry. She held the fabric up and stretched it from hand to hand. "We'll pin the wings to our sleeves so we can flutter them."

As Finley cut the fabric into the shape of a pair of giant wings, Henry grabbed some more pipe cleaners. "I'll make some antennae for you."

"And I'll get some safety pins for the wings," Olivia said. "My skirt was too big, so we had to pin it. I brought extras just in case."

Olivia went to her desk and came back with a handful of safety pins. She held the fabric in place while Finley pinned it along Henry's sleeves.

Finley stood back to look. "Presto change-o! You're ready to fly!"

Henry lifted his arms and spread his wings. "I'm ready for a vacation," he said. "Let's make like monarchs and head to Mexico."

"Wait for me!" Finley said as Olivia pinned on her wings.

"Not a bad costume," Olivia said, admiring her work, "considering it was Plan C."

"I know what could make it even better — a chrysalis!" Finley put on her antennae and handed Olivia the extra mosquito netting. "Could you wrap us up?"

"I'd be happy to," Olivia replied. She cut the leftover netting in two. She wrapped one piece around Finley and the other around Henry.

Just then Ms. Bird rang the chime. "Fourth graders, it's time for the parade! Form a single-file line, and we'll head to the auditorium."

Finley scooted into line behind Olivia. Henry squeezed in behind Finley. Ms. Bird straightened her top hat, grabbed her wand, and led the class down the hall to the auditorium.

As they got to the door, Finley peeked in. The stage lights were on, and the younger grades were already in their seats.

That's a lot of kids, Finley thought, *even with second grade gone on the field trip.*

Finley's class lined up behind the other fourth-grade classes, and students started filing across the stage one at a time.

Ms. Bird paused as they reached the stairs. "Don't forget to smile," she reminded them before walking onstage.

The audience clapped as Ms. Bird pulled scarves, plastic flowers, rubber chickens, and what looked like a live snake out of her hat. Every time she waved her wand, a cloud of glitter drifted down. Then she bowed and sashayed off the stage.

"Wow," Henry said. "That's a hard act to follow."

Suddenly, Finley had an idea. She whispered in Henry's ear as the line moved forward and students took their turns onstage.

Will waved his light saber and posed like an action figure. Tyra demonstrated her ninja moves. Olivia waved a hand around her crystal ball and curtsied.

Then it was Finley's turn. She shuffled out to the middle of the stage and waited. Henry shuffled out next to her.

They squirmed and wiggled, loosening their netting little by little. When her chrysalis fell to the floor, Finley spread her wings.

"Flutter by, butterfly!" Henry told her.

Finley ran in a wide circle, fluttering her wings, and Henry followed. Then they snatched up their chrysalises and flew across the stage as the audience clapped.

When they'd made it down the steps and into the aisle, Henry gave Finley a fist bump. "That was awesome! I felt like Houdini escaping from my chrysalis."

"Your wings looked so cool!" Olivia said, giving them each a high five.

"I like your monarch costumes," Ms. Bird said as they exited the auditorium. "Very creative."

"Thanks," Finley said. "Sometimes it pays to have a Plan C."

When they got back to the classroom, everyone headed for the snack table. Finley turned to Henry. "Should we grab some Halloween treats?"

"Maybe just a couple," Henry said. "I'm planning on having lots of candy tonight trick-or-treating."

Trick-or-treating. Finley had almost forgotten. She had to track down Evie and get Henry his real costume in time.

"Uh-oh," she said. "I just remembered — Evie's riding home with Lucy from the pumpkin patch. I'll call you as soon as she gets home with our *real* costumes."

"Mom's taking me to get new soccer cleats after school," Henry said. "I have a game tomorrow, and my toes are about to bust out the front of my old ones. But my dad will be home if you want to drop mine off."

"Okay," Finley said. "I'll bring it over as soon as I can. Then you'll have time to get dressed up and hand out some candy before you come over to trick-or-treat."

"Sounds good." Henry grinned. "Vampire Elvis is ready to rock 'n roll!"

Chapter 10
WE'VE GOT SPIRIT

When she got home, Finley changed out of her butterfly costume and sat on the porch, waiting for Evie to arrive. Dad came out of the garage carrying an armload of fabric and dumped it under the maple tree in the front yard.

As Finley watched, he threw a rope over one of the high branches. Then he attached a fabric ghost to the end so it bobbed in the breeze. Two more ghosts lay on the ground at his feet.

"Hey!" Finley called. "What are you doing?"

Dad glanced up. "Raising my *spirits*!"

"Ha," Finley said. "Very funny. When are Evie and Mom coming home?"

"I don't know," Dad said, "but I could use some help. We need to get these decorations up before the sun goes down."

"Okay," Finley said. "What do you want me to do?"

Dad tied the last of the ghosts to the tree, then held up some plastic skeletons. "Evie wanted mummies," he said, "but these'll have to do. They were on sale — two for one. Follow me."

Finley hopped down from the porch and Dad passed her a skeleton. Together they carried the dangling decorations to the trees on the other side of the yard. Finley laid hers on the grass and helped Dad stretch some wispy fabric between two trees.

"That looks like a comfy place to stretch out," Dad said, tying the fabric to make a gauzy hammock. "Ready, Mr. Bones?"

Finley grabbed the skeleton's head, and Dad held its feet as they lifted it in. Then he dragged

an extension cord over and plugged in two strings of orange lights.

"Let's drape these around him," he suggested. "Then he'll glow in the dark."

As Finley started arranging the lights, Evie came bounding across the lawn with two big bags. "We got more lights on the way home!" she said, passing the bags to Dad.

"Thanks," Dad replied. "How was the field trip?"

"Good." Evie grinned. "I picked a pumpkin and named her Penelope. She's on the porch."

Finley put her hands on Evie's shoulders and looked into her eyes. "Evie. *Please* tell me you have my bag."

"Oh." Evie looked at her shoes. "Yeah, sorry about that. I must have grabbed the wrong one."

Finley groaned. "We didn't have our costumes for the Halloween parade."

"I didn't *mean* to take them," Evie said. "I thought your bag was mine. Besides, I was missing my stuff too."

Finley glared. "Where is it?"

Evie frowned. "In the kitchen."

Finley raced inside. She unzipped the bag, rifled through it, and breathed a sigh of relief — it was all there. Now she just needed to get Henry his costume.

"I'm headed to the store to get candy!" Dad called in the front door. "Anybody need anything?"

"Yes!" Finley answered. "Could you drop something off at Henry's?"

"Sure," Dad said.

Finley put Henry's costume in a bag and handed it to Dad. "Thanks," she said. "He needs it for tonight."

"Sorry again," Evie said, peeking through the kitchen doorway.

"It's okay," Finley told her. "It wasn't your fault. We'll put our names on the outside of our gym bags so it doesn't happen again. By the way, what was all of that stuff in *your* bag? The marshmallows, the bug spray, the garlic, the toilet paper . . ."

"My haunted corn maze survival kit," Evie said. "Just in case."

Finley couldn't help but smile. "I'm glad you didn't need it."

Evie grinned. "Me too."

* * *

When Finley went back outside, Mom was pounding a sign into the lawn that read: *HAUNTED! Enter at Your Own Risk.* She wore a red, white, and black dress and a red wig. Her face was pale and powdery, and her lips were painted in the shape of a heart.

Finley tiptoed closer to get a better look. "Mom?"

"You mean, your majesty?" Mom said with an English accent. "After all, I am the Queen of Hearts."

"Sorry, your majesty," Finley said. "You look amazing."

Mom struck a pose. "Why thank you, my dahling!"

Finley helped Mom tie up the other hammocks, and Zack and Evie came out just in time to tuck in the rest of the skeletons. Finley stretched hers out in one of the fabric hammocks and tilted its head like it was peering over the edge. Zack propped his up in a sitting position holding a tangled ball of lights.

"Look, mine's doing the splits!" Evie said.

Just then Dad returned wearing a White Rabbit costume and carrying an armload of candy.

"Wow," Evie said, staring. "I like your whiskers."

"Thanks." Dad held up a hairy, black spider decoration and a bag of cotton gauze. "I'll get the pumpkin-carving stuff ready. But first, who wants to make a spider web?"

"I do!" Evie said, grabbing the spider and the bag.

Finley followed her to the porch. They tugged and stretched and wrapped the gauze around the porch columns to form a giant web. Then Finley hung the spider in the middle.

"There," she said. "She's ready to catch a tasty treat!"

"Or a tasty trick-or-treater!" Evie said. "Are you going to carve your pumpkin?"

"I just got it," Finley told her. "I'm not ready to carve it. Maybe I'll save it for a Thanksgiving centerpiece."

"You can help carve mine," Evie offered.

Just then, Dad came out of the house with a stack of newspapers, a bowl, two spoons, and a knife. "Let's do this before it gets dark," he said, spreading the newspapers out on the porch. He pulled out a marker and handed it to Evie. "You design, I carve."

Evie drew two big eyes and passed the marker to Finley. Finley sketched a wavy circle for a mouth with two teeth on the top and one on the bottom. Then Evie made a triangle nose.

"Stand back!" Dad said. He carefully cut out the eyes, nose, and mouth, then cut a wide circle around the stem. He handed the pumpkin to Evie. "Let's see what's under that lid."

Evie yanked on the stem, and the top came off, trailing tentacles of orange goo. "Yuck!" she said, giggling. "Pumpkin guts."

Dad handed Finley and Evie each a spoon. "Scoop out the seeds and put them in the bowl," he said. "We can roast them later."

Finley and Evie both went to work scooping out the pumpkin's pulpy insides. They finished just as the sun sank below the treetops.

Finley looked out on the yard. The skeleton hammocks hung like giant cocoons, Mom's sign stood tall on the lawn, and the spider web cast a net of shadows on the porch floor.

"Wow," she said. "We've got spirit."

"Spirits," Evie corrected, pointing to Dad's ghosts, which swayed and turned on their tethers in the trees.

Finley grinned. "Now I just need to get my costume on, and we'll be ready for Halloween night!"

Chapter 11
TRICK OR TREAT

"Come grab some pizza!" Mom called from the kitchen. "No treats until you eat!"

Finley and Evie each wolfed down a piece of pizza and ran upstairs to get ready.

"Can you leave your door open?" Evie asked, lingering in the hall.

"I guess," Finley said. "Why?"

But Evie had already vanished.

Finley glanced at her clock. Henry would be over soon. She put on her leggings, shirt, and scarf. Cracking her glow sticks to activate them, she slipped some inside the skirt and pulled it on. Then she twisted her hair into a messy bun, sprayed it with sparkle dust, and finished it off with more glow sticks and Olivia's fiber-optic barrettes.

Just then Evie popped her head through the doorway. "Ooh! I love your costume."

"Thanks," Finley said. "Can you turn the lights off for a sec?"

Evie flicked the switch, and Finley turned on the bike lights and the strands of lights in her skirt.

"Awesome!" Evie said. "You're all shiny!"

Finley looked in the mirror. She was shiny. And sparkly. And definitely not a carrot. She was ready.

She flicked the lights back on and grabbed her treat bag. "Come on — let's scare up some treats!"

Dad was doing the dishes when they walked into the kitchen. "It's my favorite zombie ballerina and supernova!" he said, drying his hands and taking out his phone for a photo. "Say, 'Halloween treats, *pleeeeease!*'"

"Halloween treats, *pleeeeease!*" Finley and Evie echoed.

Dad snapped the picture. "Got it!"

Finley and Evie found Zack sitting on the porch swing, pouring candy into the tin tub Mom had set out for treats. The sun was just setting, coloring everything with a warm, Halloween-ish glow.

"Are you sure you don't want to dress up?" Evie asked him. "I have an extra tutu you could borrow."

"A tempting offer," Zack said. "But no thanks. Pass me one of those bags of candy, will you?"

Finley tossed him some taffy, then grabbed a bag of lollipops. She ripped it open to add to the tub.

"You two had better be careful out there tonight," Zack said. "That's when all the monsters come out." He made a scary face at Evie, then dumped the rest of the candy into the tub. Grabbing the empty bags, he disappeared into the house.

"Finley," Evie whispered, tugging on Finley's arm.

"Hold on," Finley said, carrying the candy tub to the porch table.

"Finley." Evie tugged again. *"Vampire."* Then she slipped inside.

Finley looked up and spotted a vampire slinking down the sidewalk toward the house. His face was white, his hair was slicked-back, and his cape flapped in the breeze.

"Henry!" she called.

Henry waved at Finley, then turned to his mom, who was waiting on the other side of the street on her bike. "Bye, Mom! See you later!" He held the edge of his cape up to his face and peered over his arm as he crept up the steps to the porch.

"Wow!" Finley said. "You look *fang*-tastic!"

Henry let his cape drop and smiled, showing his pointy, plastic teeth. "*Fang* you very much," he said in his best Elvis voice. "You should join my *fang* club!"

Finley laughed. "I love the sideburns. What do you think of the bling?"

"It's perfect," Henry said. "And you're a super-spooktacular supernova. You really light up the night."

Just then Dad came out carrying a tray of spice jars and the seeds Finley and Evie had scooped out of the pumpkin. "Hi, Henry," he said. "Love your costume!"

"Thanks, Mr. Rabbit," Henry said. "You're looking pretty dapper yourself."

Dad set the tray down on the porch table. "You're just in time to make some snacks. Toss these pumpkin seeds with a little oil and salt and whatever spices you think would taste good. I'll roast them, and you can have them for a snack after trick-or-treating."

"Thanks!" Finley and Henry said together.

Finley fished a seed out of the bowl and held it up next to Evie's jack-o'-lantern. "It's amazing something so big can come from something so small."

"Let's see what we've got," Henry said, examining the spices. "Pepper, cumin, chili powder, cinnamon, hot sauce . . . a little curry powder might be good." He unscrewed the cap and held the jar out for Finley to smell.

"Mmm," she said. "Let's try it."

Henry sprinkled some curry powder into the bowl and tossed the seeds until they turned a golden yellow.

"Maybe a little cinnamon," Finley suggested, "for a touch of sweetness."

"And a sprinkle of salt," Henry said, shaking some over the seeds. "I see you eyeing that hot sauce. Didn't you learn your lesson with the PB&J pasta you made for the cook-off? That's KA-POW-erful stuff!"

Finley laughed. "Maybe just a tiny bit?" She passed Henry the bottle. "Here, you can do it."

Henry unscrewed the cap. "A *tiny* bit." He let two drops fall and stirred them in.

Suddenly, the front door flew open. Evie leaped out, followed by Zack and Mom, who was fanning herself with a giant Queen of Hearts card.

"We're ready!" Evie announced.

"The trick-or-treat train is leaving," Mom said to Zack. "Want to hop on board?"

Zack shook his head. "I'm good. I'll stay here and give out the candy."

"Thanks," Mom said, mussing up his hair. "The White Rabbit's in the kitchen if you need him."

"Woo-hooo!" Evie bounded down the porch steps. "Let's go!"

Finley and Henry turned on their flashlights and joined the line of trick-or-treaters who were trickling down the sidewalk. Evie skipped and twirled in front of them, swinging her treat bucket.

"Don't get too far ahead," Mom called from behind.

Finley and Henry followed Evie up and down the street, filling their treat bags. They passed Little Red Riding Hood, a flapper, a bunch of hippies with tie-dyed shirts and bell-bottoms, a knight, Dorothy and the Tin Man from *The Wizard of Oz*, and Rapunzel.

Finley and Henry's treat bags were getting heavy when Finley realized she'd lost sight of Evie. Glancing back, she saw Mom talking to Mr. Greenberg from down the street.

"Where did Evie go?" Finley asked Henry.

"I don't know," he said.

Finley scanned the sidewalk. Evie was nowhere in sight.

Chapter 12
A BOO-TIFUL NIGHT

Finley surveyed the yard and street. "Maybe she's at the next house," she said hopefully.

Finley and Henry checked the next house.

And the next.

They were about to run back and get Mom when Finley heard a sob. She turned around to find Evie, her makeup smeared, tears running down her face.

"What happened?" Finley asked. "Where were you?"

"I bumped into a creepy werewolf. Then I ran and tripped and scraped my knee. I thought I was lost — until I saw your lights flashing." Evie took a ragged breath. "I was supposed to be a zombie, but I guess I'm just a scaredy-cat. I hate Halloween!"

"It's okay," Finley said. "Everyone gets scared sometimes. Come on — let's get Mom."

* * *

When they got back to the house, Dad was blaring organ music, and Zack had left his post on the porch.

"Can you turn that down a bit?" Mom called inside. "You're going to frighten the trick-or-treaters, and then we'll be stuck with all this candy."

Finley glanced over at Henry. "Maybe that's his plan."

Mom took Evie's hand. "Come on, zombie girl, let's fix up your knee."

Evie turned to Finley as she followed Mom inside. "Thanks," she said, sniffling. "Ever since Zack told me about that dumb corn-maze ghost, I've been scared about Halloween."

"He was just messing with you," Finley said. "And some of those costumes tonight were really spooky — but they're just costumes. Have fun sorting your candy. I'll trade you sour gummies for peanut butter cups."

Evie smiled. "Deal." Then she skipped off after Mom.

A few minutes later, Dad brought out the roasted pumpkin seeds. "Here you go," he said. "They're still warm from the oven."

"Thanks," Finley said, taking the bowl. Then she and Henry sat on the porch swing so they could watch the parade of trick-or-treaters.

Finley surveyed the sidewalk. "I spy an angel, a flamingo, a cowboy . . ."

"There's Cleopatra and Wonder Woman," Henry said. "And is that a caveman? Or Bigfoot?"

"Caveman," Finley said, sampling some seeds. "See his club? Mmm, these are good." She held out the bowl for Henry, and he scooped up a handful.

"There are lots of great costumes, but I like ours the best." Henry took out his fangs and popped some pumpkin seeds into his mouth. "Everything worked out great — we got to be three things for Halloween instead of one."

Finley smiled. "Way to look on the bright side."

Henry shrugged. "It's true." He pointed to a group of kids gathering on the sidewalk in front of Finley's yard. "Hey, aren't those sixth graders? That witch looks familiar. Was she at Camp Acorn with us?"

Finley nodded. "She's also in Zack's class at school. I feel bad for him. He used to love trick-or-treating, and now he thinks he's too cool for it. He's probably playing video games or something."

The group of kids sauntered down the walkway to the porch, laughing loudly.

"Trick or treat!" the witch and Wonder Woman said together, holding out their candy bags.

Finley and Henry dropped a couple of treats into each one, and the pair mumbled "thank you" before heading back down the walk. Next came a pirate and a superhero, then a gangly ghost who didn't say a word.

As the ghost walked away, Finley noticed something strange — it was wearing Zack's favorite shoes.

Finley flew down the porch steps. Before she could think twice, she grabbed a corner of its sheet and tugged.

The ghost spun around and tugged back. "Hey, watch it! You're going to blow my cover." It was Zack all right.

"Ha!" Finley said. "I knew it was you! I thought you were too old for trick-or-treating."

Zack glanced over at his friends and shrugged. "I changed my mind. I guess you're never too old to have fun."

Finley smiled. "I'm glad you got into the Halloween *spirit*. Go have fun — we'll hold down the fort."

"Thanks," Zack said. "I owe you." He ran to catch up to the rest of the group, his sheet flapping behind him.

Finley and Henry watched as the older kids moved on to the house next door. "Do you ever think you'll stop dressing up for Halloween?" Finley asked.

Henry smiled. "Not as long as I've got you to help with my costumes." He pointed to the cauldron on the porch table. "Hey, what's in there?"

"Witches' brew," Finley said. "Want some?"

Henry peered into the murky liquid, then shrugged. "I guess so."

"Don't worry," Finley said, handing him a cup. "It's just punch. Dad made it."

"Look at the moon." Henry pointed to the sky above the house across the street. "It's a *boo*-tiful night."

"There are so many stars," Finley said. "It's hard to believe they won't always be there."

Henry nodded. "Even stars don't last forever. But they'll be there for a long, long time. And when they're gone, they won't be *gone* gone — just scattered everywhere."

"We're all stars in a way," Finley said. "I read it in the book you gave me. Stardust from dying stars is recycled into planets and the things on them. Like you and me — and monarch butterflies."

Henry held up his cup. "To monarch butterflies — and supernovae and vampire Elvis and good books!"

Finley bumped her cup against his. "To all kinds of magic, big and small! And to many more super-spooktacular Halloweens!"

About the Author

Jessica Young grew up in Ontario, Canada. The same things make her happy now as when she was a kid: dancing, painting, music, digging in the dirt, picnics, reading, and writing. Like Finley Flowers, Jessica loves making stuff. When she was little, she wanted to be a tap-dancing flight attendant/veterinarian, but she's changed her mind! Jessica currently lives with her family in Nashville, Tennessee.

About the Illustrator

When Jessica Secheret was young, she had strange friends that were always with her: felt pens, colored pencils, brushes, and paint. After Jessica repainted all the walls in her house, her parents decided it was time for her to express her "talent" at an art school — the famous École Boulle in Paris. After several years at various architecture agencies, Jessica decided to give up squares, rulers, and compasses and dedicate her heart and soul to what she'd always loved — putting her own imagination on paper. Today, Jessica spends her time in her Paris studio, drawing for magazines and children's books in France and abroad.

Pick-a-Flavor Roasted Pumpkin Seeds

When carving your jack-o'-lantern, save those seeds to make a tasty Halloween treat. Ask an adult to supervise, and have fun making a super-spooktacular snack!

What You'll Need:

- baking sheet or shallow, oven-safe baking dish
- 2 cups of pumpkin seeds, washed in a colander, and dried — or store-bought, dried pumpkin seeds
- herbs, spices, and hot sauce to taste — see combinations on the next page
- sprinkle of salt
- sprinkle of sugar
- 2 tablespoons olive oil or melted butter

What to Do:

1. Have an adult preheat the oven to 350 degrees. Get out a baking sheet with a rim or a shallow baking dish.
2. Clean and dry the pumpkin seeds (unless you're using store-bought, dried seeds).
3. Toss the seeds in a bowl with olive oil or melted butter. (If you're using butter, ask an adult to help you melt it.)
4. Add the spices (see below) and salt/sugar and mix. Then spread the seeds in a pan or baking dish in a single layer to roast.
5. Have an adult put the seeds in the oven and bake for approximately 15–30 minutes. (If you're using store-bought pumpkin seeds, bake for a shorter time.) Start checking and stirring the seeds after 10 minutes to make sure they don't get too roasted!
6. When the seeds are golden brown, have an adult take them out and let them cool before eating.

Try some of these flavors, or make up your own!

- **Sweet:** cinnamon, sugar
- **Sweet and savory:** fresh rosemary (ask an adult to chop it), sugar, salt
- **Curried:** curry powder, cumin, salt
- **Spicy:** chili powder, hot sauce, salt

Giant Spider Web

Weave your own spider web sculpture! Pick an out-of-the-way spot for safety, and ask an adult to help. Most importantly, try not to get tangled up!

What You'll Need:

- balls of yarn, or spools of ribbon or tulle — at least 50 yards, depending on how big your web will be
- trees, porch columns, a fence, or other structure to anchor your web

What to Do:

1. Get an adult to supervise your web-weaving. Find two trees, porch columns, fence posts, or other structures 5–10 feet apart for anchoring your web.

2. Tie one end of the yarn, ribbon, or tulle to one of the trees or posts.

3. Stretch the yarn to the other tree or post, wrap it around once, then stretch it back to the first post, wrapping it in a new spot.

4. Repeat this process at varying heights on the posts until a "web" forms between them. Try to wrap high and low so the web will fill in evenly.

5. When the yarn runs out, or when the web is finished, tie the other end of the yarn around one of the posts to secure it.

Be sure to check out all of Finley's creative, Fin-tastic adventures!